Little, Brown and Company

Hachette Book Group
237 Park Avenue, New York, NY 10017
Visit our website at www.lb-kids.com

Little, Brown and Company is a division of Hachette Book Group, Inc.
The Little, Brown name and logo are trademarks of Hachette Book Group, Inc.

First Edition: April 2010

ISBN 978-0-316-08354-6

10 9 8 7 6 5 4 3 2 1

CW

Printed in the United States of America

THE JUNIOR NOVEL

Adapted by Alexander Irvine
Based on the screenplay by Justin Theroux

LITTLE, BROWN AND COMPANY
New York   Boston

CHAPTER 1

A massive aircraft soared through the sky. Below it, lights flashed and people screamed. When Iron Man tipped himself out of the cargo door of the plane and began soaring toward the ground, an observer might have thought he was diving into a war zone. But no...this was more like a Hollywood movie premiere.

It was opening night of the Stark Expo, a show sponsored by Stark Industries that brought together the best and brightest minds from around the world to share ideas and new technologies.

The crowd on the Expo grounds poured into

the Tent of Tomorrow. They had already been treated to a montage, on the giant video screens, of Iron Man's recent exploits: an aerial tango with a barrage of shoulder-fired missiles, a lightning raid on a pirate ship off the Horn of Africa, a head-on collision with an air-to-air missile whose explosion coming over the Expo sound system was loud enough to register on nearby seismometers. The crowd loved it.

And they exploded at the sight of Iron Man falling from the sky to execute a perfect somersault at the last moment and land at the center of the stage.

Robot arms sprouted from the stage and formed a framework around Tony Stark, unlocking the invisible joints on the Mark IV suit and lifting it away from his body. From the crowd's perspective, it appeared that Iron Man had been disassembled and a tuxedo-clad Tony Stark constructed in his place. The whole procedure took only a few seconds. Tony was a genius inventor and billionaire who had created the Iron Man suit so that he could help people and fight the evils of the world.

"It's good to be back!" he called out over the tumult. He paused for a moment to get his breath. Six months earlier, when he'd turned himself into the armored Super Hero, he hadn't known what a physical toll it would take. Between the explosions, the late nights, and the recent problems with palladium, Tony Stark was not the man he had once been. But he had a show to put on.

"Ladies and gentlemen," he began. "Decades ago, my father, Howard Stark, began a grand tradition. Every ten years, he would level the playing field for inventors by building a city. An idealized city. A city of the future. An Expo where for five glorious months, scientists, world leaders, and corporate CEOs could come together to pursue one goal: advancing mankind."

The giant TV screen behind him lit up with archival footage of the first Expo. The camera panned across visions of the future ranging from the fanciful — *Your Children's Flying Car Is Here*

Today! was one slogan that drew a laugh from the crowd—to the hardheaded and practical, all against the backdrop of the New York City skyline.

"A place to do the impossible," Tony said. "A place to unleash ideas." Howard Stark appeared on the screen, shown in his workshop sometime around 1970.

"Everything is achievable through technology," Howard Stark said in the old film footage. "Better living, robust health, and—for the first time in human history—the possibility of world peace!" He gave the camera a nervous smile as he walked to a scale model of that first Expo. "And everything you'll need in the future can be found right here. So from all of us at Stark Industries, I'd like to personally show you the City of the Future...the Stark Expo! Welcome."

Applause from the crowd swelled over Tony's father's speech. Tony himself picked up the thread. "Today I'm issuing a challenge. A challenge for anyone, any country, any company to prove its value. A chance to put up the best ideas, the best inventions...the best foot forward, in the hopes of leaving the world a better place than the one we came into." With a bow and a flourish, he headed for the stage exit. "That's all I've got for now. Have a good time!"

As he spoke the last words, the lights cut to black. The music picked up where it had left off, booming through the darkness as the crowd went nuts all over again. The Stark Expo, bigger and better than ever, was under way.

✸◉✸

In a forgotten part of Russia, a flickering television screen showed Tony Stark's grand entrance at the Expo. It was quite a spectacle: flashing lights, loud music.

Ivan Vanko watched. He was alone except for the television and his cockatoo, Irina. His father, Anton Vanko, had passed away recently. Since then Ivan had turned his small apartment into a workshop, filled with welding equipment, spools of wire, and bits of metal.

His father had told him many things—and *shown* him many things. Ivan had learned the true stories of Anton Vanko's work and Tony Stark's crimes. Ivan had absorbed as much of his father's knowledge as he could. He had sorted through old records and plans, notebooks and loose sheaves of paper covered in diagrams and equations.

Ivan shuffled through boxes of his father's papers and brought out a cardboard tube. On the peeling label he read the English words: STARK INDUSTRIES. Underneath were two names: HOWARD STARK and ANTON VANKO. It was time for Ivan to claim his heritage and for Tony Stark to learn the bitter truth about his own. Ivan returned to the worktable and spread out the blueprints in the spill of lamplight. The English words ARC REACTOR filled him with a sense of purpose. Tony Stark believed the Arc Reactor was his own invention. Ivan couldn't wait to see the look on Tony's face when he realized how wrong he was—for that alone Ivan Vanko would have given his life. But Tony Stark was arrogant and prideful, and Ivan didn't think it would ever occur to Tony that someone could be his intellectual equal.

At least, not until it was too late.

Happy Hogan was there to meet Tony as he came offstage. "How'd it go?" Hap asked.

Tony shrugged. "I've done better."

"This way, sir." Happy pointed, and they immediately headed through the wings to the backstage meeting and media area.

Tony signed a replica of an Iron Man mask for a little kid and scribbled a few other autographs. Then Happy hustled Tony down the corridor toward the backstage doors. Tony was running out of gas—fast.

"Let's get out of here," Tony said as he staggered from exhaustion. Happy grabbed his friend and held him up. Looking around to see if anyone had noticed Tony's stumble, Hap asked, "You okay, man?"

"Aces," Tony said. He'd started to notice odd discolorations around the Arc Reactor housing in his chest. Tendrils of a sickly purple color radiated out from it. Put that together with the unpredictable bouts of weakness, and he was pretty sure he had a big problem.

Tony had his artificial intelligence program, called Jarvis, trying to find a new power source for the reactor in his chest. The palladium fuel cells that currently glowed inside it were clearly poisoning him.

Happy shoved open the backstage door, and a fresh wave of shouts and flashes greeted them. Tony rose to the occasion, shrugging off Hap and playing to the crowd as they maneuvered toward the car. Happy triggered the remote control that opened the roof of Tony's favorite set of wheels—a gray sports car. Tony grabbed the key from Happy. "I'm driving," he said.

As he settled into the driver's seat, a ravishing brunette appeared next to the sports car.

"Pleased to meet you, Mr. Stark," she said.

Tony had no idea who she was. "You, too, Miss...?"

"Marshal," she said.

"I'm Tony, Ms. Marshal, and you are...?"

"U.S.," she said, and slapped an envelope onto his chest. "You are hereby ordered to appear before the Senate Armed Services Committee tomorrow at nine a.m.," she said. She let go of the envelope and turned away.

Tony turned to look at Happy, who was reading over the subpoena. "Do I really have to go to that?"

"This?" Happy said. "Yeah, I think you do."

✵◎⬡

It was not the first time Tony had testified before the Senate, but he had a feeling it was going to be the least pleasant. He was at a table by himself. His primary antagonist was a certain Senator Stern, who was currently speaking to him.

"I'm sorry we're not seeing eye to eye here, Mr. Stark, but according to these contracts, you agreed to provide the U.S. taxpayers with"— Stern flipped through a file and read—"'all current and as yet undiscovered weapons systems.' Now, do you or do you not at present possess a very specialized weapon—"

"I do not," Tony said firmly.

"You are not in possession of said weapon?"

"It depends on how you define the word *weapon*," Tony said.

"The Iron Man weapon," Stern said.

"My device does not fit that description."

"And how would you describe your device?" Stern's tone of practiced weariness grated on Tony.

"A high-tech prosthesis."

Stern became angry. "The Iron Man suit is the most powerful weapon on the face of the Earth," he said. "Yet you use it to sell tickets to your theme park."

"My father conceived of the Stark Expo to transcend the need for war by addressing its sole cause: the coveting of resources," Tony said. "Primarily energy. If your priority in this hearing was truly the safety—"

"Our priority is for you to turn the Iron Man suit over to the military."

"I am Iron Man," Tony said. "The suit and I are one."

The senator decided to try a new tactic. "I'd like to call upon Justin Hammer, our current primary defense contractor, as an expert witness."

Justin Hammer strode down the aisle. His tie was a bit loose, his pants a bit tight, his hair flopping over his forehead as he nodded at acquaintances on his way to be sworn in. He ran Hammer Industries, a huge rival company to Stark Industries. Since Tony had stopped making weapons, Hammer and his company had stepped in to supply the U.S. government. But the rivalry hadn't ended.

Tony turned his focus back to the committee. "Let the minutes reflect," he said into the microphone, "that I observe Mr. Hammer entering the chamber and am wondering if and when an expert will also be in attendance."

Senator Stern's gavel banged over an outburst of laughter. If Hammer was bothered, though, he didn't show it. "I may well not be an expert. But you know who was?" he asked, playing to the gallery but addressing the question to Tony. "Your dad. Howard Stark. A father to us all, and to the military-industrial age. And just to be clear: he knew that technology was the sword, not the shield, that protects this great nation. A sword that when rattled can calm threats from foreign lands and slay dangers before they arrive on our shores."

Hammer went on. "Anthony Stark has created a sword with untold possibilities, and yet he insists it's a shield! He asks us to trust him as we cower behind it! I love peace, but we live in a world of grave threats. Threats that Mr. Stark will not always be able to foresee."

Tony rolled his eyes. *Anthony?* Nobody had called him Anthony since maybe the first day of kindergarten, which he'd gone to only because other kids did.

"We can't let a similar technology be created by a country far less moral than our own," Hammer said. "Believe me, ladies and gentlemen, when I say that Mr. Stark keeps the secrets of that suit at the peril of our citizens."

Tony had an idea. He slipped his new PDA out of his pocket. It was a rectangle of fiber optics, pure computing power that looked like a piece of clear plastic. He started fiddling with it while Senator Stern continued. "Thank you, Mr. Hammer. The committee would now like to invite Lieutenant Colonel James T. Rhodes into the chamber."

Tony looked up, toward the door, where Rhodey was entering in full dress uniform. He looked uncomfortable.

Tony met his best friend in the aisle and shook hands with him. Tony was glad to see Rhodey there. If there was any living human Tony knew he could count on to do the right thing, that person was James Rhodes.

After Rhodey had been sworn in, Stern said, "I have before me a report on the Iron Man compiled by Lieutenant Colonel Rhodes. Colonel, please read into the minutes page fifty-four, paragraph four."

"Certainly, Senator," Rhodey said. "May I first point out that I was not briefed on this hearing nor prepared to testify—"

"Duly noted," Stern said without looking up from his notes. "Please continue."

Rhodey swallowed the snub and went on. "This paragraph out of context does not reflect the summary of my findings."

"Did you or did you not write 'Iron Man presents a potential threat to the security of both the nation and her interests'?"

By way of answering, Rhodey continued and completed the quote. "'As he does not operate within any definable branch of government.' However, I went on to recommend that the benefits far outweigh the liabilities—"

"Thank you, Colonel Rhodes," Stern said.

Undeterred, Rhodey finished his sentence. "And that it would be in our best interest to fold Mr. Stark into the existing chain of command."

"Colonel Rhodes," Stern went on, "please read page fifty-six of your report."

Rhodey glanced at the indicated page and gestured to a bank of monitors, which lit up to display blurry satellite images. "Intelligence suggests that the devices seen in these photos are in fact all attempts at making manned copies of Mr. Stark's suit." With a laser pointer, he indicated points on each of the monitors where blurry images showed something like an armored suit.

Enough, Tony thought. He fired up the mini virtual desktop on his PDA and set to work getting some visual evidence that would actually prove something—even if it wasn't what Stern and his colleagues had set out to prove.

"This has been corroborated by our allies and local intelligence on the ground," Rhodey went on, "indicating that they are quite possibly, at this moment, functional."

Tony stood and touched an icon on his PDA. "Let's see what's really going on here," he said as his PDA took control of the monitor screens. "If…I…may," he began, as a series of classified videos—some of them existing only on intranets behind security walls that the Department of Defense would never get through—loaded and began to play. At top left, a North Korean testing site was hosting a test flight of a skeletal suit. Something like Tony's repulsors fired, lifting suit and pilot into the air. "Wow, it looks like I have commandeered your screens," remarked Tony with a smile.

"And you're right," he continued. "North Korea is well on its…" Suddenly, the suit and pilot disappeared in a flash of light that overwhelmed the camera. When the image resolved, the smoking remains of the suit were being hosed down by firefighters. "Nope," Tony said. "Whew. That was a relief."

Similar results played out on the other monitors. "Let's see how Russia is doing.... Oh, dear," Tony went on. "And Japan?...Oh, I guess not. India? Not so much. Germans are good engineers. Yowch. That's gonna leave a mark." Then he froze all the looping videos except one. He expanded that image until it took up the entire bank of monitors.

"Wait," Tony said. "The United States is in the game, too. Look, it's Justin Hammer." Glancing over his shoulder at the camera crews filming the hearing, Tony added, "Hey, guys, you might want to push in on Hammer for this."

What unfolded on the single remaining video was a comic disaster. Hammer stood off to one side of the frame as a crew strapped someone into an armored exoskeleton. Obviously, it had been constructed with the Iron Man suit in mind, but Tony could tell by looking at it that the weight distributions were all wrong for the location of the propulsion systems. On the monitor, Hammer stood back and winked at the camera.

The real-life Justin Hammer in the Senate chamber looked as if he had a mouthful of spoiled milk. On the monitor bank, Hammer's prototype suit lifted off into the air over the proving ground and started a loop-the-loop that quickly turned into a spiral. The thrusters cut out with the operator moving parallel to the ground, and pieces of the prototype started to fall off. He landed in a sitting position, kicking up a huge plume of sand. Hammer could be heard yelling to cut the video.

In the Senate chamber, Hammer stood. "I would like to point out," he said, "that the test pilot survived and suffered only minor spinal bruising. He is currently white-water rafting with his family."

Senator Stern pointed his gavel at Tony. "By making a mockery of this hearing, you are short-changing the American people!" he bellowed.

Tony turned to face the camera. "The good news is," Tony said, "I'm your deterrent. The goal of the suit is not to use it. And it's working. You're welcome. I have successfully privatized world peace. Not that I'm above throwing on the suit and breaking up an international fight here and there.

"You want my property," Tony said. "You can't have it. I try to play ball with you. Something goes wrong overseas, I get the three a.m. call. My bond is with the American people, whom I will always keep safe."

And there was the gavel, hammering down as Stern said "Adjourned!" and rose to stalk off the committee dais. Tony hopped down from the lectern he'd taken over, flashed peace signs, and blew kisses. The cameras loved him.

✸◉✦

Fool, thought Ivan Vanko. He was working while watching Tony Stark's Senate hearing on television. And he was carrying on an occasional conversation with Irina, the cockatoo.

He was nearly finished.

Ivan's eyes watered and his neck ached from hunching over the fine soldering work required in the construction of a functioning miniature Arc Reactor. Until that exact moment, only two had existed in the world. Now there was a third, tiny and perfect, glowing on his worktable as if it possessed secret knowledge. This was a moment his father would have loved. Ivan wanted to share it with someone, so he reached out one hand toward Irina's perch and waited for her to climb onto his knuckles.

"Isn't it beautiful, Irina?" The bird chirped.

Ivan Vanko had made an Arc Reactor. He was the second man in history to do so. It would forever gall him that Stark was the first, that Stark had suppressed Anton Vanko's pioneering work and then taken sole credit for further developments. Ivan would have to console himself with being there when Tony Stark was destroyed.

The Arc Reactor fit perfectly in the palm of Ivan's hand. He plugged it into the ancient desktop computer he had scrounged out of the trash and ran a diagnostic program he had written. All of the Arc Reactor's processes were happening exactly as they were supposed to, within the parameters he had sought.

The Arc Reactor glowed. Irina cackled. Outside, the sun was setting, and snow was beginning to fall. Ivan began to piece together the next part of his plan.

CHAPTER 3

No good deed goes unpunished. Pepper Potts's good deed was inviting Rhodey to catch a ride on Tony's plane back to California. As Tony Stark's assistant, Pepper helped with all things relating to Stark Industries and to Iron Man. Her current assignment was to get Tony home from the Senate hearing.

Since Rhodey was stationed at Edwards Air Force Base, northeast of Los Angeles, and since he and Tony had been friends for many years, and since their friendship was currently strained, Pepper had reasoned that there were several good reasons for extending the invitation. And even knowing Tony's occasional propensity to act childish, she had not anticipated the current situation. She sat in a seat between her boss and her boss's best friend. Neither one of them would talk to the other; both were feeling betrayed. Both wanted an apology.

"This is ridiculous," she finally said. "Are you for real? Are you not going to talk for the entire flight?"

Looking at her, Tony pointed at Rhodey. "What's he doing here? Why isn't he on Hammer's plane?"

"I was invited," Rhodey said.

"Of course he was invited," Pepper said. "Rhodey is always welcome."

"Not by the owner of the plane," Tony said. "And that's bad jetiquette. Guests are not allowed to invite other guests."

Rhodey tried again. "Tony—"

"I'm not a guest," Pepper interrupted. A warning tone crept into her voice.

"Can you tell him I'm not talking to him?" Tony said.

"Then listen," Rhodey said. "What's wrong with you? Do you know that showing classified footage on national television is—?"

"No worse than stabbing your best friend in the back at a Senate hearing?" Tony broke in. "How about a heads-up next time?" He pointedly gave Rhodey the cold shoulder by turning to Pepper.

But Rhodey wasn't finished. "I gave you the report! I asked you to fact check it!" he protested.

"Did not," said Tony.

"He did," asserted Pepper.

Tony glared at both of them. "Like I would even remember," he said with a wave of his hand. "You still owe me an apology."

"I wouldn't count on it," retorted Rhodey.

Pepper interrupted before the argument could get any worse. "Tony, let's go over your schedule. Can we schedule the call with the secretary-general of the United Nations? It's embarrassing that we missed—"

"Let's talk about my birthday party," Tony said.

Pepper took a deep breath. She wondered how long it would take her to hit the ground if she jumped out of the plane at that exact moment. "I recommend that in keeping with the times, we do something small, elegant," she began.

"I don't follow trends—I set them," Tony said. "We're gonna have a huge party."

Pepper forged ahead. "Monaco," she said. "I think we should cancel." The Monaco Historic Grand Prix car race was one of Tony's favorite biennial rituals.

"Absolutely not," Tony said, exactly as Pepper had anticipated. "I've entered a car in the race." Which Pepper knew, of course. She had seen the financials on the car. Stark Industries had spent a mint on maintaining Tony's vintage race car.

"Great," Rhodey said, with enormous false enthusiasm. "I won't be there. We can 'not' have lunch together."

"What? You're not going?" Tony looked suspicious.

"I don't think we should hang out right now," Rhodey admitted. "It's bad for our friendship."

Tony looked away, out one of the windows.

There was silence as the jet began its descent. Rhodey wanted what was best for the United States, and to him the Iron Man suit was the culmination of a long tradition of U.S. military superiority driven by technological innovation. Tony was privately of the opinion that much of Rhodey's hard-line attitude about Tony's actions came from simple jealousy. Rhodey wanted a suit. It was that simple.

"Next time," Tony said, "you're flying commercial."

⊛◉☉

Once he got home, Tony went straight into his lab to work with Jarvis on testing new combinations of possible power sources for his chest repulsor transmitter. Jarvis was trying all sorts of chemical combinations in an effort to improve the formula. But the tests kept failing. The palladium was proving to be toxic to Tony's body.

"Rise in palladium levels," Jarvis said. "Biological toxicity now at twenty-two percent."

Bad news. Tony sighed as he traced the purple lines spreading from the center of his chest. They were thicker and longer. Some of them had sprouted smaller lines that wandered off to meet each other, creating a webbed effect.

He heard someone on the stairs and looked over his shoulder to see Pepper tapping her code into the access panel at the lab door. Tony quickly buttoned up his shirt and picked up one of his new inventions, a Tech-Ball, tossing it around nonchalantly as he turned to meet her.

"What were you thinking?" Pepper snapped without preamble as soon as she was through the door. Her words took Tony aback just a bit, but of course he couldn't let her know that. "Just now?" he said. "If a doughnut was the size of a washing machine, would I be able to take a bite out of it?"

Pepper ignored his reply. "Did you just donate our entire modern art collection?"

Tony had, in fact, made the donation. At least he had ordered it done, and he thought that his orders had been carried out. But because he was in a literal mood, he decided not to commit to an answer about which he could not be 100 percent certain. "I'm not sure," Tony said. "I didn't physically check the crates."

"We curated that collection for more than ten years!" Pepper said. He could tell that she was purely baffled. So was he, actually. Why had he done that? "It's worth more than six hundred and eight million dollars!" added Pepper.

Tony shrugged. This was not a persuasive line of argument. "Of *my* money."

"It's tax-deductible," Pepper said. "Why didn't you check with me?"

"Can I do it? See, I'm checking with you." Tony let the Tech-Ball bounce off the desktop.

"Check with me *before* you do it," Pepper said.

"Is it okay, then?"

Pepper gave up. "Yes, it's okay."

Tony nodded. "Good. Think fast."

As he spoke, he tossed the Tech-Ball to her. Reflexively, she reached up to catch it — but instead of slapping into the palm of her hand, the Tech-Ball turned inside out, wrapping around her hand like a cocoon.

"I don't want to play ball with you," Pepper said after a moment. The Tech-Ball turned back into a ball. Setting it down, she said, "There are a hundred other things to talk about. Which category would you like to start with? Stark Industries?"

"Not yet," Tony said.

"Iron Man," Pepper said.

Tony shook his head. "Love it, but pass." What was there to talk about? Iron Man was Iron Man.

"Expo?" Pepper asked.

Ah. That's more like it, Tony thought. He nodded. "Shoot."

"Wind farm initiative, plastic tree plantation, solar retrofitting…"

"Whoa!" Tony held up a hand. He couldn't deal with all of this right now. But he was pretty sure he knew someone who could. And she was standing right in front of him. He paused, wondering if the time was right. He decided it was.

"I'm giving you a promotion," Tony announced. "Do you accept?"

Pepper froze. Her face ran through six different expressions. "Are you serious?" she asked. Tony just blinked at her. "You...you are serious," she said. "I—yes! Yes, I accept!"

"Congratulations, Ms. Potts," Tony said, shaking her hand. He meant it.

"I have so much to do," she said. Turning on her heel, Pepper hurried from the room. Tony turned back to his palladium problem.

CHAPTER  4

After hours of more failed tests, Tony decided to vent some of his frustration by taking a boxing lesson from Happy. He'd had a boxing ring put into his home gym just for this purpose.

"Cover," Happy said, after sticking a jab into Tony's nose. "Don't drop. Hands up. Jab-jab-hook-uppercut-jab."

Eyes watering from the jab, Tony threw the combination. Happy flicked the punches aside and said, "You're dropping your hook. Again."

Tony heard the doorbell ring and a moment later looked up to see Pepper walking into the gym. "The messenger is here with the paperwork for my promotion," she said.

"Great," Tony said.

A young woman he had never seen followed Pepper into the room.

"Natalie Rushman, Mr. Stark," Pepper said. "Mr. Stark, Natalie Rushman."

"Pleased to meet you, Mr. Stark," Natalie said. "And congratulations, Ms. Potts."

Tony invited Natalie up into the boxing ring. She climbed up and tried to hand him some papers to sign. "How long have you been with Stark, Natalie?" Tony asked.

"Ah, barely six months," she answered. "In legal." Tony looked her up and down. Then he hopped out of the ring and went over to one of the many holographic computer screens he had around the house. Tony pulled up Natalie's résumé from the Stark Industries personnel files. What he saw impressed him.

Natalie held out a pen and the stack of forms, trying again. "You need to sign, Mr. Stark."

Going back to the ring, Tony nodded. He signed the papers quickly and handed them back.

"Well! It's official!" Pepper said. "Off you go, Miss Rushman, and thank you for bringing those by."

Pepper walked Natalie out and then headed back into the gym. Tony made no effort to keep the admiration out of his voice. "Did you see her résumé? Fluent in French, Italian, Russian... *Latin*? Who speaks Latin?"

"I know where this is going," Pepper said, "and no. I'll be hiring my own replacement."

"Hire *her*."

❁◎◉

Ivan could have chosen any of a thousand different ways to destroy Stark, but in the end Ivan's chosen weapon was the whip. His creation was five feet long, made of articulated tungsten carbide vertebrae. He had machined each vertebra himself and linked them together onto a woven cable. A handle, insulated and wired to the power supply, extended another six inches.

Deactivated, the whip lay on his worktable. Ivan wound copper wire around the vertebrae, weaving it along the cable and through holes like the nerve openings in a spinal column. When the weapon was done, Ivan Vanko would possess a whip of white-hot molten metal. Not even Stark's armor would survive it for long. Nothing could. Ivan finished wiring the whip. He shrugged into a harness he had built of leather-wrapped tungsten and placed the miniature Arc Reactor in a housing set over his sternum, mimicking the Iron Man chest plate.

He ran the cable from the glowing chest repulsor transmitter down his arm to the handle of the whip, attaching it at the shoulder, the bicep, and the radius. Before he plugged in the RT, Ivan put on a glove; even with the insulation, he did not expect to be able to hold the whip bare-handed. The glove extended well up his forearm and would protect him from accidental grazes of the whip.

Taking the whip in hand, Ivan stepped away from the table to a clear space in the middle of the floor. He plugged the power cable into the whip. It sparked to life with a hum that shook Ivan's bones and a crackle that he could feel pressing on his eardrums. He flicked out the whip, and bits of plasma jumped from the tip, searing holes where they landed. Irina squawked and fluttered her wings, scooting to the end of her perch farthest from the light and noise.

Glancing around the room, he caught sight of the television replaying highlights of Tony Stark's Senate hearing. Ivan flicked the whip away from his body and then pivoted to bring it down in a sweeping arc. The sight and sound of it connecting with the television was like a lightning strike with thunder. His ears rang, and his eyes watered from the flash. An involuntary grin spread across his face as he blinked away the tears and looked at what he had done.

The television now lay in two roughly equal halves; the ancient screen and tube had exploded into sprays of glittering fragments. Ivan had not felt a thing, no sense of resistance or even impact. His grin broadened. He flipped the whip in a tight loop as if spinning a lasso. The tip sparked, leaving a gouge in the floor. He touched a stud on the inside of his wrist, and the whip shut off.

Now that it was operational, Ivan decided to build a second whip.

CHAPTER 5

A few days later, Tony took all of them to Monaco
for the big car race. While Happy parked the
limousine, Tony, Pepper, and Natalie went into
a fancy hotel restaurant to watch the race. Tony
had overruled Pepper and had hired Natalie as
his assistant, and he was pleased with his decision
so far. Natalie's fluent French saved them when
they tried to order drinks from the waiter.

As Pepper looked around the room, she saw
TVs mounted everywhere, airing pre-race coverage.
Then she spied Justin Hammer walking across the
room. Tony spotted him, too, and sniffed in disgust.

"Tony!" Hammer boomed on his way to the table. Hammer inclined his head at Pepper and said, "I just wanted to pop over and congratulate Ms. Potts on her promotion."

"Thank you," Pepper said.

Hammer turned to Tony. "I'm actually hoping to have something to present at your Expo this year," he said.

"Love it!" Tony said. "Just so you know, we're mostly highlighting inventions that *work*."

"Don't count me out," Hammer said. "Maybe you haven't heard, Tony, but you're not the only rich guy with a fancy car in the race this year."

"Really? Look alive, then. I have a pretty decent driver this time around."

On the television screens, the crowd noise ratcheted up. Cars were moving into position. "Looks like we're about to see who's got the better man," Tony said. "Now if you'll excuse me, I'd like to freshen up before the ball."

Tony zipped out of the room before anyone

could stop him. It was race day! Tony was ready to enjoy it.

$$\circledast \odot \circleddash$$

Hammer had wandered to another table with some business associates. He glanced up at the TV to see whether the race had started. What he saw on the screen made him gasp.

On the screen, in high def, big as life, was Tony Stark, getting into a car with the Stark Industries logo on it. He was suited up like the other drivers. He settled into the car and placed the steering wheel just the way he wanted it.

Hammer's mouth dropped open, then clamped shut. He couldn't believe that Tony had upstaged him again!

On the television, Tony winked and shot a thumbs-up at the worldwide audience, then roared off toward the starting line. The English-speaking announcers noted that the world was going to find out whether Tony Stark could drive a race car as skillfully as he designed and built them.

Although he couldn't understand a word of French, Hammer could hear tone of voice in any language, and he could tell that the French announcers were going crazy. He heard another gasp across the room and noticed that Pepper had just seen the television screen, too. She must not have known about it.

That Tony Stark, thought Hammer, *really knows how to keep a secret.*

CHAPTER 6

How Ivan loved machines. All machines. In Ivan's veins ran the blood of a born engineer. His father, too, had been destined for engineering greatness. A Stark had derailed that plan. Ivan would get it back on track.

Engines roared to life around him. He faded into the crowds of technicians and journalists who stood back, their jobs done for the moment, and watched the drivers run last-minute checks. One after another, the cars headed to the starting line.

As the race began, Ivan got ready, putting on his harness and two whips. When the time was right, he threw off the overcoat he'd been wearing and strode directly toward the track.

His left-hand whip slashed through the chain-link fence under the grandstand as if it weren't there, leaving a gouge in the sidewalk. Two more flicks of the whip, right and left, opened a section of fencing so that Ivan could walk through it. He came to the safety barrier bordering the track, a three-tiered metal railing that offered little more resistance than the chain link had. He slashed a V-shaped opening through it as one of the cars thundered by, the wind of its passage rocking Ivan and blowing his hair across his face.

❀◉☉

In the hotel restaurant, viewers saw that the TV cameras were focused on the disruption on the racecourse. Someone had invaded the track and was using a kind of electrified rope to hack away at the passing cars. He was big, with long, lank hair and a kind of metallic exoskeleton frame that linked his two—ropes? cables? whips?—to a power source that glowed at the center of his torso.

"The Monaco Historic Grand Prix is making history for quite another reason," said the lead announcer. "Who is this guy? He must be stopped!"

Cars were crashing into each other and piling up around the invader as they tried to avoid him. "That can't be good," Pepper said. She was trying to figure out how he was doing whatever he was doing. Then she saw that the guy on the track wore what looked suspiciously like a miniaturized Arc Reactor.

Happy walked in. "What's going on?" he asked.

"Where's the football?" she said quickly. He held it up—an aluminum briefcase lacquered in the same deep red as the Iron Man suit. They had given it the code name "football." It was shackled to his arm.

Pepper stood. It was time to make sure Tony

wasn't in over his head, for the millionth time. She told Natalie to arrange a plane to get Tony out of the country fast, and then turned to Happy. "Let's go."

Hurrying to the limo, Pepper said, "Give it to me." Happy handed her the key and held out his arm so she could reach the lock on the football. She worked at it as they ran together out of the hotel and toward the VIP lot.

The briefcase held a lightweight "travel" version of the Iron Man suit. They'd never done a field test of it, but Pepper thought this might be the time. Now if only she could get the key to work. "Hold still, Happy," she said.

"What, and run at the same time? You try it," Happy said, but he held his arm steadier as they ran. When they got to the limo, Pepper still hadn't opened the lock. With one arm, Happy drove in the direction of the track while Pepper jerked the football around, this way and that, trying to unlock the handcuff that was attached to his other arm.

"Drive faster!" she said. "And hold still so I can get this key to work."

✸◉⟲

Left behind in the restaurant, Natalie spoke into her cell phone. "He's going into turn ten."

She looked around to confirm that Hammer was riveted by the escalating mayhem on the track, and that Pepper and Happy had left the room.

While she talked on her phone, Natalie tried to track what was happening on the racecourse with Tony. "He is extremely vulnerable at the moment," she said.

She was extremely vulnerable at the moment, too. Her support network was a long way off, and it would be very easy for a misunderstanding of her operational role to escalate, compromising her mission. That could not be allowed to happen.

Natalie held the phone, listening for another moment, and then said, "Understood," and hung up. After allowing herself to relax for a moment, she dialed her phone again. The one thing she could do at the moment was make sure that the Stark Industries plane was ready to go when Tony was.

❀◉❂

Oblivious to the disruption on the track, Tony was racing around the course, having the time of his life. He had just passed Hammer's car and knew that the driver would be looking at his rear bumper for the rest of the race. He smiled.

Suddenly, he saw the cars in front of him veer crazily away from something in the center of the track. Just before one of the cars disappeared in a fireball, Tony could have sworn he saw a man… and something sparking, like live wires.

The fireball cleared, and Tony saw that there *was* a man on the track, walking against the direction of the race. He was big and muscular. From his hands dangled a pair of whips that glowed and sparked as he flicked them against the concrete.

The car in front of Tony braked and swerved. Tony stayed behind it, using it as a shield. A flickering line of energy shot out and destroyed the car, splitting it just behind the seat. The two parts of the car, spitting vapors and flame, tumbled into the crash barrier. Now Tony really pushed on the brakes, but there was no way he could avoid the guy on the track. He hauled on the steering wheel, felt the car shudder into a skid, and watched in what felt like slow motion as the guy flicked one of the whips toward Tony's car.

The whip sheared through the chassis and split the car into two pieces, which slid along the track. Tony came to a stop, upside down in the front end of his car. He popped the steering wheel loose and flipped it out onto the track so that he could wriggle out of the driver's seat. His helmet had cracked in the crash, and he stripped it off. The remains of his car rested between him and the guy with the whips and the metal exoskeleton.

At that moment, Ivan reached the wreckage of

Tony's car and slashed it methodically into small pieces, the whole time shouting in a language that sounded to Tony like Russian. Tony waited for just the right moment, then grabbed hold of the nearest bit of wreckage and swung it at the back of Ivan's head.

Tony put everything he had into the swing. It was a good one. The blow landed solidly...but had no visible effect.

Tony paused, switching tactics to psychological diversion. "Are we beyond talking this through? Finding some common ground?"

The whip guy roared like an animal and slashed at the space recently occupied by Tony Stark. But Tony was already off and running, looking for cover. All he saw were pieces of race cars, beautiful machines turned into expensive junk.

One car lay upside down at an angle that would provide brief cover. Tony ran from the whip guy quickly enough to stay alive but slowly enough to keep the pursuer coming. Then Tony dove under the car. He yanked off the gas cap and scrambled forward, away from the stream and splash of high-test fuel.

There was gas everywhere, and a crazy guy approaching with whips that apparently made fire. Tony got away just as the whip guy was close enough to strike.

The whip slashed down through the car's engine and into the track surface, coming into contact with the spreading pool of fuel. The explosion that followed blew the car to unrecognizable pieces and sent Tony pinwheeling into a wall of hay bales at the edge of the track. He started to right himself and looked back toward the dissipating fireball.

There was the whip guy, walking through the flames as if they weren't there and coming toward Tony as though he were the only thing in the world that mattered.

✦◉✦

"I see Tony!" Happy cried out. He had charged through the gate and had driven onto the track. He and Pepper were moving against the direction of traffic—but there was no traffic anymore. There were hulks of destroyed cars, pit crews running onto the track to save drivers, spectators rushing up and down the stands in waves. There was fire on the track, everywhere.

Happy lost sight of Tony. A fireball on the track hid everything. Happy floored the limo and headed that way.

"I think I have it!" Pepper yelled, still twisting at the lock on his wrist.

There was Tony again.

Happy took in the situation all at once. Tony was down, half-buried in a collapsed pile of hay bales on the inside of the crash barriers. He was moving, though. A big area of the track near Tony was on fire. Through the fire came the big nutcase with the laser whips, cracking them on the pavement and grinning at the sound.

There was one thing to do, and Happy did it. He cut the wheel hard and hammered down on the brake, sending the limo into a fishtail spin and smashing the bad guy with the back end. The limo slammed hard into the crash barrier, crumpling the railings and setting off the air bags. The vehicle came to a rocking halt, still running. It had pinned the guy to the wall.

What to do next? Happy wondered. He was about to open the door, when he noticed the boss approaching the limo.

"You got the football?" Tony asked before Happy had a chance to lower the window all the way down—but it didn't really matter, since the spider-webbed glass disintegrated as soon as he hit the button.

Pepper finally popped open the lock and raised the briefcase to show him.

"Thanks," Tony said.

"You're welcome," Pepper managed.

As Tony reached for the case, the car lurched. The maniac reared up from behind it and, with a barbaric yell, whistled one of his whips past Tony's head. The whip tore through the armored hood of the car as if it were aluminum foil. Tony spun away. The whip guy slashed at the car to free himself. He hacked away at the trunk and the rear tires, his whips even slicing into the backseat.

From the limo, Pepper called out, "Tony!" She opened the door and slid the football across the slick pavement in his direction. Then she and Happy ran from the track.

Incredibly, the lunatic whip guy, who was wearing—could it be?—an RT on his chest, had hacked away enough of the back end of the car that he was almost loose. He kept at it until, with a final heave, he shoved free of the limo's bumper and stalked through the wreckage after Tony.

By the time he reached the billionaire, however, the situation had changed dramatically. Tony caught the football and entered a code into a pad next to its handle. It chirped its acceptance. He opened the case and placed one foot in either half. Then the football proceeded to build a light, portable version of the Iron Man suit, the Mark V, from the boots up around Tony's body. It wasn't the same as the full apparatus, but it was still a formidable piece of body armor.

The first crack from an energized whip left deep scoring in the suit. Tony dodged the next several swings and goggled at the RT on the whip guy's chest. *How is that possible?* Tony thought. The glowing RT and the Arc Reactor technology were so Stark-proprietary that even the Department of Defense had never touched the tech. Who was this guy who had just shown up in Monaco and started wrecking the place with his RT-powered whips?

A whip sparked across Tony's torso, coming dangerously close to his own RT. Tony grabbed the arm holding the whip and flung the guy into the smoking wreckage of two cars. He pounded the whip guy every time an opening arose. He barraged him with pieces of cars, pieces of track, anything close at hand. Tony got in close and delivered punches until he could feel the heat from the whips. He danced away, then started the attack again.

His heart was pounding. He was tired. *Time to end this*, Tony thought as he dove into a clinch with the villain, pinning him down and just plain pounding him until the guy quit. Breathing heavily, Tony tore the RT from the whip wielder's chest and looked at it. He couldn't quite believe what he saw.

Suddenly, police swarmed the lunatic destroyer of the Monaco Historic Grand Prix, who smiled as the officers dragged him away. "I win," he said to Tony.

Tony walked off the track, looking at the RT, fascinated by it. It shouldn't have been possible, but there it was.

"Pepper," he said, "we need to get to the plane and test this."

"Test it? This is the most important thing we can do right now?" Pepper replied.

"As a matter of fact, it is," Tony said. "See, that's because this thing cannot exist. Because if it exists, that means someone out there has access to either my servers or my brain. Neither of those things should be possible. Perhaps we can find out what really has happened, once our Russian pal is interrogated. But if he doesn't tell the police anything," Tony said, holding up the RT, "this will. So, yes, we need to test it. Okay?"

"Okay," Pepper said.

CHAPTER 7

By the time Tony walked into the local police station, he'd run some preliminary tests on the RT recovered from Whiplash — as the media had already named him — and the results were startlingly similar to Tony's own design.

In the hallway, Tony Stark stopped a French prison official who was on the phone. "...Russian, but he speaks English," he was saying. "No. All we got was a name."

When the official hung up the phone, Tony asked, "Who is he?"

"Not sure yet. We're assuming he's Russian."

Tony tried to think of any Russians who might want to put together energized metal-filament whips to hurt him — *and* who might be able to build an RT. None came to mind. "I need to talk to him," Tony said.

The official let Tony into the holding cell where a manacled Ivan — Tony had caught the prisoner's first name on his way in — sat with his back to the door. Ivan was a big man, even without the RT apparatus and the whips.

"Is that you, my friend?" Ivan said softly. Tony didn't answer. Ivan shifted his weight but didn't turn his head. "Tony Stark?"

Tony walked around to where Ivan could see him. He held up the RT. "It's pretty good," Tony said, and meant it. "Where did you get it?"

As Tony spoke, Ivan's eyes drifted shut, and he tipped his head back. A smile spread across his face. "You like it?" he said. There was no mistaking the pride in his voice. "I'll make you one."

"You didn't make this."

Ivan's smile got a bit wider. "It wasn't so hard."

Tony took a step toward Ivan. "Who made this?"

Opening his eyes, Ivan looked Tony in the eye and laughed. "Your technology is built from stolen goods. You come from a family of thieves."

A family of thieves. Tony stored away that statement. What did this Ivan know about his family, or think he knew? "Where did you get it?" he asked again.

"It came from the past. From Anton Vanko," Ivan said reverently.

"Who's that?"

Suddenly enraged, Ivan surged against his manacles. "It is a name you should know!" he shouted.

"Why?"

Ivan cooled off. The ethereal smile returned, now with a bit of a predatory edge. "It's killing you, isn't it?"

He knows, Tony thought. How could he know? This was a problem Tony had never thought he would encounter: someone else independently arriving at tech he'd thought was his own. Well, his father's; the initial designs for the Arc Reactor came from old blueprints Tony had found in his father's lab after the old man died.

He looked back at Ivan and saw that Ivan was studying him.

"It's. Killing. You." Ivan touched his forehead, at the temple. "I know these things."

For one of the few times in his life, Tony Stark was speechless.

The French prison official entered and held the door. "Time's up," he said.

Ivan leaned his head back and closed his eyes again. He seemed happy. "Good-bye, Tony Stark," he said.

❋◎⊘

Three hours later, a guard arrived at Vanko's cell door and tapped on it to let Ivan know to stay back while he opened it.

IRON MAN

MARK I
Specs: bulletproof,
flight capable

JARVIS TAKE US ONLINE!

MARK II
Specs: flight boosters in boots, onboard computer run by Jarvis

ALL SYSTEMS GO!

MARK III
Specs: new paint job and
suit materials, ice shield

MARK IV
Specs: more aerodynamic
and streamlined design

MARK VI
Specs: new repulsor
technology, super strength,
and sonic flight

WEAPONS
ENGAGED!

ARMOR UP!

WAR MACHINE
Specs: based on the Mark II suit;
augmented with military
targeting equipment, munitions,
and air-to-air missiles

The guard looked up and down the hall to make sure it was empty. For a moment Ivan thought there would be a fight, and that was fine with him. Then the guard set down a tray next to Ivan, caught the prisoner's eye, and nodded. *Ah, Ivan thought. An unexpected twist to events.*

"Eat up," the guard said in Russian. Then he left, locking the cell again.

Ivan took a look at the food. Mashed potatoes—but it didn't smell like mashed potatoes. The next thing Ivan noticed was something he initially thought was a digital clock with a malfunctioning display. It said :30. Then it said :29, then :28...and Ivan put it all together. He knew what the mashed potatoes were, and he knew what this small LCD device was, and he understood why the guard had left it all here, and he knew that if he didn't act now, he was going to die.

The detonator read :24.

Ivan slapped the mashed potatoes up against the wall and stuck the detonator in the center of the gooey mass. It said :17. He turned back to the door just as the guard opened it. Ivan followed the guard down a hallway.

Just as they ducked into a stairwell, the charge went off back in his cell. A thunderous boom echoed through the prison, creating a perfect distraction. Sprinklers kicked in, soaking Ivan to the skin as he headed down the stairs at the guard's direction.

Who was this benefactor? Ivan could not think of a single person on Earth who could reasonably be expected to take a risk on his behalf.

Three floors down, Ivan came to a fire escape door. And he was free.

CHAPTER  8

Back at Stark Industries, Rhodey had arrived to talk to his friend. Pepper and Natalie were busy fielding calls from the press, and they waved him down to the lab.

Rhodey got to the bottom of the stairs and peered through the glass walls. Tony stood at his virtual desktop, with a blizzard of holo-projected files walling him off from the rest of the lab. He wasn't looking at Iron Man schematics or breakdowns of engines, though. He was pulling gigabytes of old video footage, photographs, scanned-in reports.... Rhodey couldn't quite see how they fit together, and he wouldn't find out until he asked, so he knocked.

Tony glanced up and let him in.

"You okay?" Rhodey asked.

"Yeah," Tony said. "Jarvis, start tapping the grid in New York."

"You look awful," Rhodey said, partly to provoke Tony and partly because it was true. Tony ignored him.

"We need to talk," Rhodey said. "That guy has changed the game. Someone else has your technology. You need to share the suit with us."

"There's no problem!" Tony said, too loudly. "The guy was a one-off. Jarvis, what's the holdup?"

"That guy was beating you in real time," Rhodey said. "You said it's twenty years before someone else would figure out your technology, but that guy had it yesterday. You need to make a statement."

Tony nodded and started moving. Rhodey followed him up the stairs and into the kitchen, where they could hear the ongoing media disaster from the living room. "You're going to have to issue a press release," Rhodey said. "Soon."

"Sure thing," Tony answered.

Tony walked outside and hailed a news helicopter that was circling his house. "Hey!" he shouted. "Iron Man won! That guy was toast. The world is safe! Iron Man is back on watch!"

Rhodey rolled his eyes. "Really?"

"I think it was effective," Tony shot back.

Rhodey looked at him with annoyance.

As they walked back into the house, Tony finally got serious and put his hand on his friend's arm. "No one understands better than I do the value of what I own. Caving in at this moment and giving over my tech would be a betrayal of what it represents. The government doesn't need my suit. What it needs are more guys like me, not more suits like mine." Tony let go of Rhodey's arm but maintained eye contact. "I created the suit to keep the peace. You need to trust that I take that very seriously."

He waited for Rhodey to say something. When Rhodey didn't, Tony added, "We good?"

"Yeah," Rhodey said, and he mostly meant it. "I think I just needed to hear you say that."

"Cool. I'll see you at my party," Tony said.

❋◉☉

Tony was true to his word. His birthday party was a huge event. While the celebrities and other guests started to arrive downstairs, Tony was still up in his room. He had asked Jarvis to run another test on his RT. "How we doing, Jarvis?" Tony asked. "Am I really healthy, or just really really healthy?"

Jarvis gave it to him straight. "Biotoxicity is at its apex. Further strains placed on your body will result in almost certain d—"

"Thanks." Tony cut him off and stood there absorbing the news. Maybe he should have programmed a kinder personality into Jarvis. It was harsh to hear words like that. Depressing. He felt angry and stood there stewing until he heard Natalie calling from one of the walk-in closets.

"I can't find it," she said.

Tony rallied. "No problem," he called back. "Bring anything."

"There are sooo many," she said, carrying an outrageously bright-colored tie. She looped it around his neck and started tying it. "Voilà," she said, buttoning his collar and tightening the tie perfectly. "I'll go downstairs and make sure everything is ready," she said, flipping open her phone as she left.

"Thanks," Tony said. "You're a gem."

※◎⊖

Natalie had seen the discoloration spreading across the upper part of Tony's chest and the base of his neck and had put two and two together. Was the RT doing something to him? If so, he was going to need some serious technical assistance, and there weren't too many people who could provide it. She made a phone call and started talking. There were people who needed to know about the situation—and who needed to be ready to take action.

❄ ◉ ❧

A while later, Pepper walked into the party, taking in the huge crowd and the fast beat. She sighed and made her way through the packed house, looking for Tony. She found him in the kitchen showing Natalie how one of his Iron Man gloves worked.

"Happy birthday," she said. "I was just stopping by."

Having freed the gauntlet from Natalie's hand, Tony was now putting it on his own. "Nonsense," he said. "We're going to dance."

Which was the last thing in the world Pepper wanted right then, but as usual Tony got his way. The music had segued into something slow, and they walked onto the dance floor.

Before the song ended, Rhodey appeared, carrying a wrapped gift.

"Happy birthday," Rhodey said, handing it to Tony.

Tony flipped the gift up into the air and blew it apart with a repulsor blast from the glove he was still wearing, showering nearby guests with glass fragments. Rhodey stared at him in shock.

"I don't need gifts," said Tony.

Tony walked off, gesturing to spin up the tunes again. Something techno and bouncy got the partygoers hopping, but Pepper and Rhodey didn't join in. They stood, motionless, in the middle of the dance floor. Around them the party surged anew. Pepper looked in the direction in which Tony had gone.

"I can't... I just don't know what to do, Rhodey," Pepper said. "Tony is not himself. He's using his suit as if it were a party favor."

"It can't be this way," Rhodey agreed. "It's not safe."

Pepper bit her lip.

"I can handle this," he said. "Go home. I'll take care of it." He watched her walk toward the door, saying brief good-byes to acquaintances as she went. Then he approached the sound system and turned off the music.

"Okay," he said, his voice booming into the sudden silence. "It's twelve-oh-three, so Mr. Stark's birthday is officially over. Now it's just another Tuesday. Get out."

People muttered to each other. Most of them started moving in the general direction of the door.

Then Tony, wearing the Mark IV Iron Man armor with the face shield up, reappeared in the partygoers' midst. "Party is over! After party starts now!" he cried, and a cheer went up. Tony seemed determined to act irresponsibly for the evening.

That was it for Rhodey, though. *Decision time*, he thought. Rhodey turned and left the room. He was about to do something that Tony might never forgive, but for the life of him, Rhodey couldn't figure out what else to do. He remembered Tony saying that what people needed was not more suits like his but more guys like him. Right now, Rhodey held the opposite opinion. One Tony Stark was plenty. More than enough, in fact.

But one Iron Man suit was not enough at all. Not nearly.

Tony turned to see something he'd never thought he would see. There stood Rhodey, in Tony's own Mark II gray metal suit, in Tony's own house, embarrassing him in front of his guests.

"Time for bed," Rhodey said. He looked serious.

"You know that's mine, right?" Tony said.

Rhodey nodded. "I do."

"Just checking," Tony said.

He slapped Rhodey's arm away and gave him a two-handed shove into the opposite wall. With a thrust-assisted spring, he caught Rhodey before he could get back to his feet; their combined weight and momentum was too much for the wall, and they blew through it into the gym.

They grappled in the boxing ring. Tony uprooted a corner post and swung; Rhodey got one of his own, and the two of them went at it like broadsword-wielding medieval knights until the posts were too bent and broken to be useful anymore. Then Rhodey blew Tony through the wall with a repulsor blast, and the fight moved on to the bedroom. Tony went after Rhodey again, and the two of them crashed through a walk-in closet and the wall behind it, bursting into the kitchen in a flurry of punches. Tony finally collapsed in a pile of armor, and Rhodey was left standing.

Rhodey's head ached from the impacts on the suit's helmet, and his body felt like one big bruise. He flew away from the ruins of Tony's house in the suit, knowing that his actions would change the nature of their friendship—maybe even end it. Forever.

He had wanted to believe Tony's spiel about

being committed to using the suit for the right reasons and protecting it from those who shouldn't have access to that kind of technology. The world would have been a better place if that were true. But the world wasn't like that, and Tony Stark was not that kind of man. Rhodey could be sad and disappointed about it, but he knew his duty.

Edwards Air Force Base was ninety miles away. Rhodey called ahead, using a direct line to Major Julius Allen. Their conversation was brief. When he landed in a hangar at Edwards fifteen minutes later, the major was still yelling at everyone in sight. "I want this entire area on lockdown!" he shouted at a lieutenant. "Get those guys out of here! I want only necessary personnel!"

Rhodey flipped up the suit's face shield and walked toward the major, who saluted him.

"Major," Rhodey answered, with a nod. "Let's talk inside."

CHAPTER 9

It was morning. Tony didn't like mornings, as a general rule. Warnings from Jarvis about the dangers posed by palladium poisoning, and the certain knowledge that Rhodey had betrayed him to the generals who would turn the Iron Man suit into...whatever they were going to turn it into, were making this particular morning worse. The only thing making it bearable was the box of jelly doughnuts in his lap.

Tony wasn't sure how he'd gotten into his bathrobe or who had delivered the doughnuts, but he knew who had demolished the kitchen—himself.

He didn't want to think about it. He munched on a doughnut instead.

"Mr. Stark," someone called from the living room. "I'm going to have to ask you to please put down the doughnut."

"I got five more," Tony said, with a mouthful of jelly.

"Don't make me come in there," the man said as he entered the kitchen. The stern-looking African American wore an eye patch and a black leather jacket.

"Oh, brother," Tony said. "Aren't you the guy I kicked out of my house a while back?"

"We were going to have this conversation sometime," said the bald-headed man. "Now seems like a good time."

Tony shook his head. "Not interested. I have a lot on my mind." He turned his attention back to his doughnuts.

After a brief silence, Eye Patch tried again. "How about I buy you a cup of coffee?" he said pleasantly.

Tony was intrigued. Ten minutes later, fresh coffee was brewing in Tony's fancy coffeemaker. Good thing it had survived the previous evening's fight.

"Who are you again?" he asked Eye Patch.

"I'm Nick Fury."

Tony vaguely recalled the name, but he stopped trying to remember where he'd heard it before when his assistant, Natalie Rushman, walked in and poured the coffee for him. She was dressed in a dark navy blue bodysuit. She looked tough as nails.

"Cream and sugar," she said, setting down the cup in front of him.

Tony looked back and forth between Natalie and Fury.

"Pleased to meet you, Mr. Stark," Natalie said. "My name is Natasha Romanoff."

Natasha Romanoff? Tony took that in. So Natalie was not what she seemed. "Good assistants are so hard to find," said Tony. Especially assistants who weren't really spies.

"I was asked to keep an eye on you," she said. "To *protect* you. I'm sorry I lied, but I needed a cover so I could stay close to you without arousing suspicion."

It sounded good, but Tony still wasn't sure he could trust her. Or Nick Fury.

"Tony, I'm the executive director of S.H.I.E.L.D., the Strategic Homeland Intelligence, Enforcement, and Logistics Division," explained Fury.

Tony nodded. He remembered hearing that before. "Want a tip? Fire your namer of things, because that's a mouthful."

"Our namer of that particular thing is dead," Fury said.

"Problem solved," Tony said. Then he sipped the coffee.

"Your father named the organization," Fury said.

Tony opened his mouth, then shut it again. He didn't want to believe it, because if he did, he had to believe some other things about his father that didn't quite square with the image of Howard Stark that Tony carried around in his head.

Fury was looking at him. "Have I got your attention?" he asked. "Your father was one of the founding members of S.H.I.E.L.D. There are a lot of things you don't know about him. Things about yourself, too."

Tony sat down in a chair. He gathered his bathrobe around him and said, trying not to overreact, "I know all I need to know about myself."

"Oh, really," Fury said. "And what's—"

"I'm dying," Tony said. He pulled back the lapels of the robe to show Fury the discoloration and skin eruptions that now spread from the RT all across his chest and shoulders.

Fury looked closely. "Your body is rejecting it?"

"*It* is rejecting my body," Tony corrected him. "The tech is strong. I'm the weak link. I'll be dead by the end of the year."

"Time to get better, then, Iron Man."

"Believe it or not, I've already looked into the getting-better thing."

"And?"

"I would prefer it. But it's not an option."

"It's the only option," Fury said. "You're Tony Stark. You built that suit. You said you were Iron Man. Like it or not, you're the future. And unfortunately, the future is a lot bigger than you. Time to cowboy up."

He put something on the table while still looking Tony in the eye. Tony glanced down and saw a roll of sixteen-millimeter film and a manila envelope. "What's this?"

"You ever wonder why you built your Expo?" Fury asked.

Unable to help himself, Tony opened the envelope. Inside it was a black-and-white photograph of a fortyish man taken sometime in the 1950s or early '60s, if the surrounding tech was anything to judge by.

"Who's this?" he asked.

"Anton Vanko," Fury said. "He worked with your dad."

Whiplash's father! This was a curveball. "I

didn't see this in my files," was all Tony could think of to say.

"Because it was in *our* files." Fury paused to let that sink in. "Your father was working on things bigger than just weapons for the military," he went on. "Your father saw the future. Which is why he came and worked for us."

"What do you mean?" Tony asked.

"Sometimes people are born before the world is ready for them," Fury replied. "Leonardo da Vinci invented the helicopter before anyone had even predicted flight. Howard Stark made a few predictions, too. He was just born way too early to execute them. The world had to play catch-up. And now we're here."

Tony had always believed that his father was a genius. But to hear his father mentioned in the same breath as Leonardo da Vinci...that was strange. Tony wasn't sure how to react, and he also wasn't sure what Fury meant the comparison to convey.

"What do you mean?" he repeated.

But Fury had given him all Fury was going to give him. He tapped a finger on the film canister and said, "The world has just caught up. Howard's grasp was a lot bigger than his reach." Fury stood. "That's where you come in. And if you don't, someone else will."

CHAPTER 10

Ivan's mysterious benefactor flew him to the United States and was funding his work. This person had an entire fleet of drones—and all Ivan had to do was build RTs for them.

Ivan took it all in. One week earlier, he had been working in two rooms with illegally tapped power and a computer he'd scrounged from someone else's trash. Now he was looking at perhaps three thousand square feet of gleaming white space. There were more computers than he could imagine needing to use. At a glance, he saw tools for smelting, machining, welding, wiring, plating, microwave circuit manufacture…all types of building processes, large and small. *If my father had been given the use of a lab like this*, Ivan thought, *he would have changed the world*.

But Stark had taken away that glory. It was now up to Ivan Vanko to reclaim it.

Much of the lab's floor space was taken up by long rows of gleaming metal drones, humanoid in shape and visibly armed. Ivan walked to the bank of computers that lined one wall of the lab. Before he could make any decisions about the drones, he needed to know how they were put together.

While the data compiled, he examined one of the drones. It had a humanoid exoskeleton, with a large empty space inside the torso. The drones were his soldiers. They needed some work, but they would do nicely.

One of these, Ivan thought, *will be the last thing Tony Stark ever sees*.

Unless—and this was the only more desirable possibility—the last thing Stark saw was the apparatus Ivan Vanko was building for himself.

A staff sergeant gathered a select group of Air Force engineers who had been waiting in the machine shop attached to the hangar where the Mark II lay on a table. Rhodey, with Major Allen at his left, stood next to it and nodded at the engineers as they came in. These were the Air Force's best and brightest combat engineers, together with a few lab guys who were there to glean what technological goodies they could while they were putting together the new version of the suit.

"What you will be weaponizing," Rhodey told the assembled team, "is a flying prototype of the Iron Man Mark II, for the purposes of an offensive footing."

"Yes, sir," the engineers said, more or less in unison. The engineers approached it, wrenches and screwdrivers in hand. One of them picked up the helmet.

"Don't forget," Rhodey said. "This thing was made by Tony Stark. You're not going to learn everything." He unscrewed the suit's RT and held on to it, just in case. "We're just arming it."

As the engineers got to work, Justin Hammer slammed in through the machine shop door and walked straight to the Mark II.

"You have got to be kidding me!" Hammer exclaimed with excitement. "I got here as quickly as I could."

Rhodey shook hands with Hammer and said, "You think you could hook it up?"

While they were greeting each other, Hammer's men were bringing in an array of crates and setting them near the Mark II.

Hammer winked and popped the lid off the closest crate while his men opened the rest. Before them was a huge array of weapons, including what looked like a miniature cruise missile with onboard continuous command-and-control systems.

Rhodey looked it all over. "Done deal," he

said, after a brief—and calculated—pause. "Get busy."

"Which ones do you want?"

"All of 'em," Rhodey said on his way out of the hangar. All of a sudden, he had a lot to do.

❈◎❖

Tony Stark was a collector of outdated technologies. Luckily, one item in his collection was an old sixteen-millimeter film projector. Tony spooled the film Fury had left for him, and started it up.

"Everything is achievable through technology," Howard Stark said, just as he had on the archival Expo footage Tony had shown at the new Expo's opening ceremony a couple of weeks earlier. "Better living, robust health, and for the first time...sorry...the first..." He burst out laughing. Getting himself back to his mark, he waited while the film crew got ready to do the shot again.

Off camera someone said, "Okay, and action, Howard!"

"Everything is achievable through technology," Tony's father began again. He trailed off. After about five seconds, the crew started to chuckle.

"I'm sorry, Ron. Let's finish this tomorrow," Howard said.

"Cut," said the off-camera voice. The screen went blank...

...and then came to life again, with a pajama-clad Howard Stark in his laboratory with an Expo model behind him and a baby cradled against his shoulder. It was dark, and much of the lab was in shadow. "This is the third night you've kept me up with your crying," said Howard Stark to his son. "Thought I'd give your mother a rest. Right now you haven't mastered English yet, so I thought I'd put this on film for you," Howard went on. "I want to show you something."

He stepped aside to let the Expo model fill

the frame. "See that? I built that for you. Some-day you'll figure it out. And when you do, you'll achieve even bigger things with your life. I just know it. You're the future."

Nick Fury had said the same thing. Only not in the same way. Tony started to shake off his sentimental response and engage his intellect. This footage was his father sending a message, and he expected Tony to figure out what it was.

"I've created so much in my life, but you know the thing I'm proudest of?" Howard was talking to the baby Tony, but now he looked directly into the camera. "You. My son."

Yeah, Dad, Tony thought. *I love you, too. What are you trying to show me?*

And there it was.

There it was! Something at the edge of the frame caught Tony's eye. Scrambling in the semi-darkness for a pen, he jammed it into one of the projector's spindles, stopping the film. Watching carefully, his entire mind focusing on the puzzle his father had sent him, Tony wound the filmstrip back manually, frame by frame, until he saw it again.

Behind his father was the scale model of the first Expo he had used when pitching the project to the relevant authorities in New York City. Something about the shape, the organization of the buildings…it went with what his father was saying. Tony wound the film slowly, slowly enough that he could see each of the still frames and check the tiny differences between them.

There. Tony leaned forward, tracing his finger along the edge of the frame.

At the moment Howard Stark was saying "the future," the shape was clear. The structures looked as though they were arranged the way the atoms might be arranged in a certain molecule.

"He knew," Tony said. "Jarvis, I'll be right back."

Tony ran to the office to grab the Expo model and was back in a flash. He set it up in the lab. On the virtual desktop, he projected an image of the film frame at the end of his father's outtake—the one with the partial image that had begun to make the shape, and his father's plan, clear to him.

Looking at it, Tony realized the lab setup he had wasn't going to do the trick; the power draw was going to be immense, and he had a hunch he was going to need a lot more computing power than was available in the house network.

Tony went out to the garage and came back draped in cables and carrying a sledgehammer. He dropped the cables in a pile, closed his eyes for a minute to dredge up the memories of how he'd wired the house, and then looked at the wall in front of him.

"Jarvis," he asked, "is this a load-bearing wall?"

"No, sir," Jarvis said.

Tony tightened his grip on the sledgehammer and started swinging.

CHAPTER  11

Forty-eight hours later, the Mark II was transformed.

"I think you will be very impressed," Rhodey said as he walked with General Newcomb into the hangar, where the major and the crew of engineers were assembled. "Major Allen, would you mind doing the honors?"

Allen saluted and walked to the tarp that hung from a frame of two-by-fours. After a glance back at Rhodey, he pulled down the tarp with a flourish. All present caught their breath.

The suit had the burnished silver hue of the

original Mark II, but now the outline bristled with weapons. Rhodey ran through the specs: heads-up and communications capabilities derived from highest-grade military packages combined with the existing protocols Tony had built in during initial development. Arming this suit was the next step in maintaining peace. At least, that's what Rhodey tried to tell himself.

"Unbelievable," General Newcomb breathed. "What do you even call something like that? It's like a…"

"It's a war machine," Rhodey said.

At first Newcomb couldn't take his eyes off it. After a while he managed to tear himself away from the War Machine and get down to the business of asking the kind of questions generals were supposed to ask. "Is it functional?"

"One hundred percent online," Rhodey answered.

"Good." Newcomb faced Rhodey and Major Allen. "The Pentagon has asked that I issue your first orders. Hammer is doing a weapons presentation at the Stark Expo," Newcomb said, cutting Rhodey off with a look. "We'd like to introduce the suit."

The problem, of course, was that when Rhodey had brought the Mark II to Edwards Air Force Base, he had done so with the understanding that the military was creating—in terms both Tony and Justin Hammer had used—a shield rather than a sword. General Newcomb, by making the War Machine a centerpiece of Hammer's presentation at the Expo, was redefining its function. He was turning the War Machine into an aggressive threat instead of the behind-the-scenes trump card Rhodey had intended.

"With all due respect, General," Rhodey said, "I feel strongly that we use the suit only when absolutely necessary."

"Colonel, the world needs to see this," the general said. "Fast. I assure you it is absolutely necessary."

Rhodey said nothing.

"It's also an order," the general finished.

And that was the end of the conversation. "Yes, sir," Rhodey said.

"And very nice work, gentlemen!" General Newcomb beamed at the assembled team. "You've made your country proud."

✪ ◉ ◒

Tony was using the shape of his father's Expo model as the basis for an entirely new molecule. He was trying to create something from nothing, so Tony had rigged up a crazy system to ramp up enough power. The parts included a set of mirrors designed to focus anything that hit them on a single, specific point in space; a cube of pure glass whose position in space included the specific focal point of the set of mirrors; a high-energy laser array with beams focused and intensified by the mirrors; and, finally, a centrifuge designed to spin and initiate high-energy reactions. The system was complicated—but that's why Tony Stark was a genius.

He ran checks, and everything was exactly according to specs. The only thing left to do, really, was run the experiment and see whether it would work. Could he create a new type of molecule?

"Jarvis, spin up the nonferrous centrifuge," he said, and then added, "Be ready to capture whatever floats through it." As Jarvis spun up the centrifuge, Tony ran through his internal checklist again. He'd performed every step. If this was going to work, he'd find out now.

"Let 'er rip," he said.

The laser array flared to life, first in a deep red and then modulating in frequency well up into the ultraviolet range.

"Fingers crossed," Tony said.

The centrifuge hit its target acceleration. Tony was about to tell Jarvis to spike up the energy delivery of the lasers, but Jarvis knew the experiment better than Tony did. Jarvis had already carried out the command before Tony could speak it.

Zap!

Tony was holding his breath. The lasers had gone cold, the centrifuge had spun down to silence, and the glass cube at the center of it all sat in a sterile enclosure with a tiny grain of imperfection at its center.

Tony exhaled, long and slow. "That's it, Jarvis," he said. "Scan it."

"Dissecting now."

"As soon as you get its atomic structure," Tony said, "tell me what the name—"

"Unknown element," Jarvis said. "Contains similar transgenic properties to the chemical compound vibernum. Also has characteristics known in uranium. Suggested denomination for the periodic table: Vb thirty-two."

This was good. This was what he had hoped for, even though he wasn't yet sure it would save him. "Name it," Tony commanded.

"Vibranium," Jarvis said, with as much emotion as he ever displayed about anything.

Perfect, Tony thought. "Project it!" he said. A

three-dimensional image appeared on the desktop, endless interlocking triangles joined into a perfect sphere.

"It's beautiful," Tony said. "Gimme an RT." An RT diagram appeared. Tony tinkered with it, creating interfaces with the new molecule and seeing how it all fit together. "Spin it," he said. It spun and emitted light. Tony started to think that he might actually have done the impossible. "This might actually work," he said, and set about finding out.

❁◉❁

Several hours later, he had managed to cobble together a new triangular Arc Reactor and a sleeve that went inside the existing RT socket. He set the RT against the rim of the socket. It fit. It looked good.

"Jarvis, what do you think?" he said.

"Eminently triangular, sir," Jarvis said.

It gleamed, with the vibranium power source generating roughly twice the power that the previous palladium compound had provided—and with less than 5 percent of palladium's troublesome leaching property.

"Teleconference incoming," Jarvis said.

"Who is it?"

He glanced aside to set the new RT out of the field of the teleconference view and saw the screen open out of the corner of his eye. "What do you want?" he said, not caring who it was on-screen.

Then he saw the face of Ivan Vanko, now known as Whiplash. Tony could see that he was in a workshop or lab. A mess of wires and computers was visible behind him.

"Tony," Ivan said, "today is the day the true history of the Stark name will be written. As thieves. At your own Expo, the world will learn what kind of criminal you really are."

"Let me tell you, Ivan, as one guy with daddy issues to another," Tony said. "I don't think this day is going to turn out the way you want it to. At the end of it, I'm still going to have the Expo and Stark Industries."

"Today, Stark," Ivan said, and then cut the connection.

CHAPTER 12

Natasha was sick of playing Natalie, but Fury had said in no uncertain terms that Pepper Potts was not to know of her undercover infiltration. So here she was, with a headset and a clipboard, waiting around the entrance to the Tent of Tomorrow for Pepper to show up and sit down. Hammer's demonstration was due to start in fifteen minutes.

The Tent of Tomorrow was a tent in name only. In reality, it was an open auditorium space under a soaring glass roof, with a high-tech stage and an even higher-tech backstage setup. The backstage area was swarming with Hammer Industries tech personnel making last-minute adjustments to their imminent demonstration. The front rows of seats were packed except a few chairs reserved for VIPs.

Natasha scanned the crowd again.

"Ms. Potts!" she called out. Pepper and Happy saw her and started in her direction, moving with the crowd. "How was your flight?" Natalie asked when they were close enough to not have to shout.

"Fine, thank you," Pepper said.

"I'll wait for you right here, Ms. Potts," Happy said. "Call if you need anything."

"I'll show you to your seats," Natasha said. Her phone rang, and she answered it without looking at the number. "Natalie Rushman."

❊◉❂

Tony called Natasha while he was installing the new RT in his chest, so he skipped the teleconferencing visuals. He didn't want anyone to see his chest. Purple and black streaks radiated outward from the old RT, covering Tony's torso and crawling up his neck like bad tattoos. Sometimes when he looked at them he thought they might be moving.

Natasha answered as Natalie, still pretending to be the innocent assistant instead of the lethal S.H.I.E.L.D. operative.

But it was the S.H.I.E.L.D. operative Tony needed.

"Ivan's up to something," Tony said before she finished saying hello. "He called me from a lab. Looks like it's in a warehouse complex somewhere near the Expo."

There was the barest of pauses. "Yes, Ms. Potts has just arrived," Natasha said briskly. "Okay. I'll be right there."

She must already be at the Expo, Tony thought as Natasha hung up. *Good*. Maybe she could get the S.H.I.E.L.D. personnel who were undoubtedly creeping around the place to slow Whiplash down. Or at least be on the lookout for whatever he was planning.

Tony needed to suit up and fly to the Expo, and quick. But before he could do that, he had to get the new RT into his chest. The palladium toxicity in Tony's body had reached a point of no return. If the new RT didn't stabilize everything and give him enough strength to let his immune system start to purge the palladium, then Tony Stark was not going to make it.

And that idea was intolerable. "Jarvis," Tony said, "let's get ready to swap in this new toy. How does that sound?"

"Marvelous, sir," Jarvis said.

Tony plugged it in.

At first, he felt as if someone had sent a mild electric shock through his entire body. His heart thumped back into action, and blood started moving through his veins again. And then he felt strong.

He turned to look at himself in the

mirror—and watched as something extraordinary happened. The purplish streaks darkened to a pure black. Tony's eyes popped.

Then the black streaks became fainter and began to turn silver. The silvery color of the RT appeared to spread along the pathways where the infection had been. Then the streaks were gone.

"I did it, Dad," he whispered. There was a silence, until Jarvis broke it.

"How do you feel, sir?" the AI asked. It was an empty question, really. Tony was sure Jarvis had already run a dozen screens on Tony's metabolism and overall health without Tony's awareness.

Even if the question was motivated by simple politeness, Tony appreciated it. After all, Jarvis had been there when none of the humans of Tony's acquaintance were. Which was, of course, his fault…but now was not the time to dwell on that.

"Alive," he said.

CHAPTER  13

After her phone call with Tony, Natasha left Pepper in the front row and headed for the exit, a
plan already forming in her mind. On the way she
made another call. Nick Fury answered on the
first ring.

"Fury," she said. "Tell Agent Coulson to lock
down the Expo."

Happy saw her coming, and she hung up before
Fury could ask any questions.

"Hey," Happy said.

"I need a ride," she said. He caught the urgency
in her voice and fell into step with her.

✳◎✦

Happy drove the limo while Natasha changed into her S.H.I.E.L.D. uniform in the backseat. S.H.I.E.L.D. had traced Ivan's call to a warehouse just outside the city. Natasha Romanoff was hoping Whiplash would be there. She wanted to fight him.

But first she had to deal with Happy, who still didn't know her real name.

"So," Happy said, "I've seen you having these mysterious phone conversations for the past few weeks, and now you're changing into some sort of secret-agent outfit....So why don't you level with me?"

Natasha decided to be direct. "You want the truth, Happy? I'm a secret agent working for an organization called S.H.I.E.L.D." Natasha kept talking as she zipped up her boots. "I was deployed to Stark Industries because your boss's behavior is endangering the Iron Man suit and the

American people. The agency sent me to L.A. to keep an eye on Tony and to make sure that someone was there to call in the cavalry if things got out of hand. Now step on it, Happy," she said. "Come on."

"I think maybe I'm going to stop driving people around," Happy said as he floored the limo's accelerator. He quietly accepted Natasha's explanation without questions. She was relieved.

Before the limo came to a complete stop outside the main access gate to the warehouse complex, Natasha had already opened the car door. "Wait here," she said.

"No way," Happy shot back. He turned off the ignition and got out of the limo. "You're not going in there alone."

She gave him a pitying look. "Please. Not now."

Coming around the front of the car, Happy shook his head. "'No' is not an answer I'll accept."

"Fine," she said with a sigh.

Happy was about to ask how they were going

to get into the warehouse, when Natasha walked up to an electronic access pad next to the front door and tapped in a code, as if she owned the place. She glanced at him, anticipating his question. "S.H.I.E.L.D.," she said.

Inside, they headed across a broad, multistory atrium — the part of the building that was for show — and reached the part of the building where the work happened. The lab looked like any other lab or hospital in the world: sterile surfaces, neutral colors. Lots of signs telling which way to go, lots of cameras detecting who went where. "How do you know — ?" Happy began.

"Where Vanko's lab is?" Natasha finished for him. "A little birdie told me."

They turned a corner and ran smack into a security guard doing his rounds. Happy's instincts kicked in before he knew it.

"You go ahead — I got this guy!" he said. "I'll be okay! Go."

She started to say something but then ran

down the hall, deeper into the building, before the guard could stop her.

Happy squared off against the guard, ready to box. He hooked, he fired straight rights, he went high and low with combinations...and he realized that, unlike a lot of big guys with gym muscles, the guard could take a punch. Happy nailed him with everything he had, and the guard stayed on his feet.

Happy finally landed a solid punch, and the guard was knocked out.

"I did it!" Hap said, breathing hard. His hands felt as though he'd spent the afternoon sparring with a brick wall. *Time to find that girl and make sure she hasn't gotten herself into more trouble*, he thought. Happy turned to start after Natasha but stopped short in surprise.

The entire length of the hall floor between where he stood and where she waited impatiently was strewn with the unconscious bodies of at least a dozen other security personnel. Happy looked from Natasha to her handiwork and back, unable to believe that she had handled all these guards in the time it had taken him to knock out one guy the old-fashioned way.

"Come on!" Natasha said. To her credit, she didn't comment about his boxing skills or complain that he had made her wait.

Inside the lab there were discarded prototype drones, bits and pieces of Arc Reactor models, a complete machine shop, and an incredible mess. Unused or broken parts lay on tables or where they had fallen on the floor. Cables, conduits, and hoses ran from here to there all over the space, with no visible system or guiding principle. Computers were left on, their screens displaying information that in any reasonable security regime would have been hidden away.

She dialed Tony. "He's gone," she said.

CHAPTER 14

Back at the Expo, Pepper watched as Justin Hammer strode across the polished stage to the microphone.

"Iron Man," Hammer said. "An invention that grabbed press headlines the world over. Today, though, the press has a problem on their hands. They're about to run out of ink." He arrived at center stage. "Today I give the world Lieutenant Colonel James T. Rhodes and the War Machine!"

From the ceiling, a platform descended to reveal War Machine. Pepper caught her breath.

The War Machine suit was brute strength, shining silver in the spotlights. A million flashbulbs went off.

Pepper knew that Rhodey was inside the suit. She knew, too, that he must have fought the decision to exhibit War Machine at the Expo. He was a soldier, but he did not love war; he loved his country. Like Tony, Rhodey believed that the Iron Man armor was best used only as a weapon of last resort.

Pepper could feel the adulation wafting from the crowd, and she could see Hammer eating it up. "Nifty stuff, right?" he said. Then, in a more sober tone, he added, "But in a truly perfect world, men and women of the United States military would never have to set foot on the battlefield again." Music built, and Hammer stepped around Rhodey to the lip of the stage. "Ladies and gentlemen, today we cross the threshold into…a perfect world."

Red, white, and blue smoke erupted around the stage as four lines of armored soldiers marched in perfect rhythm into the Tent of Tomorrow and stopped in formation along the sides of the stage. An announcer boomed out the name of each branch of service as its members appeared in turn: "Army! Navy! Air Force! Marines!"

When they met in their formation, slowly and in unison, the thirty-two soldiers pivoted and raised their right arms in a salute to War Machine.

And that was when Pepper — along with everyone else in the Tent of Tomorrow — realized that these were not armored soldiers.

They were walking, synchronized, remote-controlled drones.

Pepper had never heard a noise as loud as the roar of approval from the crowd. Each group of drones was colored like the dress uniform of the service branch it represented, and each had particular design tweaks. The Air Force drones were equipped to fly, with winglike additions to every limb and active control surfaces along their backs. The Army drones were squat and loaded with heavy weaponry. The Marine contingent was a bit leaner than its Army counterpart; the Marine drones looked ready to storm a beach right then and there, if only an enemy could be located. And the Navy drones stood streamlined and potent, midnight blue, racked and bristling with missiles that looked capable of turning an enemy fleet to scrap metal in seconds flat.

Then, with timing so precise that Pepper later would wonder whether he had planned his arrival exactly this way, Iron Man appeared.

Tony rocketed down through the hole in the roof in his new Mark VI suit, complete with a new triangle on the chest to match his lifesaving RT.

Whatever Hammer felt at seeing Tony crash his big party, he was a showman, and he rolled with it. "And that's not all!" Hammer said. "Here, ladies and gentlemen, is our very special surprise guest: Iron Man!"

Tony waved to the crowd while he popped open a communications channel from his heads-up display to Rhodey's HUD inside the War Machine suit. "Really?" Tony said. "A big gun on the shoulder? What ever happened to aesthetics?"

HUD to HUD, Rhodey said, "Tony—"

"That's mine," Tony said.

"It still is."

"These drones are trouble," Tony said. "Next time do your homework."

"What are you talking about?" Rhodey asked.

Tony sent him a quick scan of the drones flanking him on all sides. They were pretty well put together, and without a doubt would be a tough fight for anyone who wasn't in an Iron Man suit, but whoever had done the primary design work hadn't cared much about hiding the specifics of the power systems.

While Tony waited for Rhodey to assess what Tony had sent him, Hammer made it clear that his enthusiasm for his special guest was flagging. "Now, if Mr. Stark would step aside..."

"Oh, my goodness," Rhodey said. He had just realized what Tony already knew. That RT Tony took off Ivan Vanko in Monaco, and all the RTs in these drones?

The same.

"Go home," Iron Man told War Machine. "It's about to get ugly."

Then he commandeered the Tent of Tomorrow's loudspeaker and said, "Ladies and gentlemen, this pavilion is currently closed to the public. In an organized fashion, please find the nearest—"

He paused as he heard a ratcheting click and turned to find War Machine's heavy machine gun aimed right between his eyes. "Don't point that thing at me," he said.

"Tony," Rhodey said, HUD to HUD. "Go."

In unison, all thirty-two drones on the stage pivoted away from War Machine, dropped their salutes, and focused their array of weaponry on Iron Man.

Hammer, edging toward the wings, called to one of his technical support staff. "What is going on?"

"We're not doing it!" the tech said.

At that moment Iron Man shot upward, and the eight Air Force drones followed him, shattering the glass dome of the Tent of Tomorrow into a blizzard of slivers that rained down onto the crowd.

❀ ◉ ⬡

"You want to do this?" Tony yelled as he did a series of barrel rolls and zigzags through the Expo. War Machine stayed hot on his tail. "Let's do this!"

"*I'm* not doing this!" Rhodey yelled back. "You need to get out of here." Rhodey was a prisoner inside the suit, without any control. And the suit was going after Tony!

Not likely. "Jarvis, drone him," Tony said.

"Unable to penetrate the firewall," Jarvis said, almost apologetically.

"Do something, man!" Rhodey said.

Tony gritted his teeth. "I'm trying," he said.

The Air Force drones, meanwhile, had spread out into a kind of double-wing formation, staying tight on Iron Man. The drones were smart, well programmed, and designed to function smoothly as a team.

"So," he said to Rhodey over the comm-link. "Still happy you ran off with my suit?"

"You want to talk about this *now*?" Rhodey said.

"No. But since this army of drones might actually succeed in shooting my suit down, it struck me that maybe you and I should clear the air." Tony dodged rounds of fire—some of which came from War Machine's rotating-barrel cannon. "See what I mean?"

"I'm not doing that," Rhodey said.

"You're flying around in the suit that's doing it," Tony said. "Jarvis, can you get control yet?"

"The situation is less than ideal, sir," Jarvis said. "But you may rest assured that I'm making the very best of it."

"Hey, Rhodey," Tony said. "Did I ever tell you

that I was having trouble with the RT and that I was about to die because I couldn't figure out how to power it without using a substance that was slowly poisoning me?"

"As a matter of fact, you did not," Rhodey said.

"Well, it's true," Tony said. "I just thought I would let you know that I got it all figured out, and it's all good now. I'm not going to die."

"Terrific," Rhodey said. At that moment the War Machine suit fired off a missile, and for a while Tony was too busy to talk.

CHAPTER 15

A large crowd gathered in a pavilion outside the Tent of Tomorrow, and another group watched from a balcony across the Expo's main thoroughfare. All attendees agreed: it was one of the best shows Tony Stark had ever put on.

The excitement lasted until the moment when the eight Army drones in formation marched out of the Tent of Tomorrow's front entrance. They extruded stabilizers from their legs, like the legs that come out from the sides of a crane to keep it steady. Then they deployed heavy guns from racks on their shoulders and aimed the weapons skyward. The drones waited, making minuscule movements that tracked the progress of Iron Man and War Machine as they moved across the sky.

Then, as the aerial show wound back over the main Expo grounds, the Army drones fired simultaneously into the air.

Around the Expo's entrances and exits, S.H.I.E.L.D. personnel appeared. Their orders were to intercept Ivan Vanko.

Pepper tried to exit the Tent of Tomorrow through the main entrance, but a guard directed her away. "Some of those robots are out front there, ma'am," he said, pointing with his flashlight toward a hallway that curved around the outside of the auditorium. "You should use the side door, over that way."

She came out of the tent into chaos. Fires were burning in some of the Expo's buildings.

Tony thundered overhead, low enough that she felt the bruising wake of his passage. Firing wildly, the Air Force drones came close behind, with Rhodey an unwilling passenger in their midst. Around Pepper the world dissolved into explosions. She dropped to her knees. When everything had passed, she looked around again, amazed to still be alive.

"Was that Pepper?" Tony yelled.

"Ms. Potts was indeed in the vicinity recently," Jarvis replied.

"Tell me she's okay, Jarvis."

"Certainly, sir," Jarvis said. "Would you like me to ascertain the truth of that statement first?"

"My display just zoomed on her," Rhodey cut in. "She looks fine."

"Your display?" Tony said. *Why would—?* he wondered. *Ah. That explains some things.* Tony knew that Ivan had designed the power source for the drones. He therefore assumed that Ivan also had programmed the drones and War Machine to seek and destroy Iron Man. If Ivan was controlling Rhodey's systems, he might also be the party responsible for checking on Pepper's status—which meant that he viewed Pepper either as a target or as leverage. That was a problem.

Right now, though, Tony's immediate problem was the eight drones on his tail. He peeled into a high loop, slowing down ever so slightly. The Air Force drones closed in. He wanted to keep them close and keep their fields of fire angled away from the evacuating crowds. He hoped to spring a little surprise when the time was right.

Tony wasn't sure which feature of the Expo was his favorite: the Unisphere, reconstructed from the original built for the first Stark Expo, or the artificial lake Tony had added as a reflecting pool. Two hundred feet tall, the Unisphere rotated on a solar-powered pedestal assembly. The globe's longitude lines were I-beams, and its structural integrity was guaranteed by the stainless-steel continents and archipelagos that adorned it. A massive STARK logo stood out above the continents, angling from south to north across the Unisphere's equator.

All of this went through his mind as he flew in

a high arc over the lake. War Machine was hot on his trail. "Jarvis, we need to get a handle on War Machine's operating system," Tony said.

"Displaying architecture," Jarvis said. A graphic rendering of the information architecture of the War Machine suit appeared on Tony's HUD.

Rhodey broke in. "What's going on up there, man?"

Tony dipped close to the surface of the lake, letting the violent currents of his passage kick up rooster tails of water to confuse his pursuers. At the same time, he swerved through a series of tight loops and figure eights. He lost a couple of the Air Force drones but found himself facing three others across the length of the lake. They were steaming toward him at full thrust. The least he could do, Tony reasoned, was reciprocate the gesture.

The impact with the center Air Force drone was not too bad. A little shudder through the frame of the suit, a brief whiteout in the visual sensors, and then Tony was through the blossoming fireball. The Unisphere loomed in his sights, and the surviving Air Force drones—some of them, anyway; they were moving too fast for a reliable count—were closing in on his tail again.

But War Machine was closer. Tony ran a targeting projection on the Unisphere.

"This might hurt," he said to Rhodey.

"What? No, you are not—"

The way Tony had it figured, War Machine—and therefore Rhodey—was tight enough on his burners that any calculations that worked for Tony would work for Rhodey, too. The Unisphere rotated slowly.

The Mark VI Iron Man suit flew through a gap in the rotating sphere, with War Machine close behind. Tony's calculations were correct: he and Rhodey got through safely. The Air Force drones, however, didn't make the move fast enough; they smashed into the sphere.

✺◉�)

Pepper saw the explosions and was nearly sick with worry. She took out her phone and called Tony, who answered on the third ring. "Ms. Potts," he said, "I told you never to call me here."

"I just wanted to—"

Pepper heard impacts through the phone. "Ouch," Tony said. "Gotta go. Bye."

He clicked off. That's when she saw him reappear through the smoke billowing up from the Unisphere, with War Machine a few yards behind and what looked like two Air Force drones flanking them. War Machine was firing with everything it had except the big missiles. Whatever the reason for not deploying those, Pepper was glad about it.

✺◉☽

Coming in low and hot back over the lake, Tony thought briefly that he'd lost the Air Force drones. Only War Machine showed up on the pursuit radar. Scanning the HUD for drones, Tony was shocked when he was jerked downward by War Machine grappling along his back. The gray metal suit had caught up with him. War Machine wrenched Tony off course and sent both of them scraping along the side of a building, peeling off a floor's worth of windows and a long line of steel framing.

"Aaaah!" Tony cried out. "I will remember you did that."

They shot clear of the building, out toward the edge of the Expo grounds. Tony braked hard, pivoting him and War Machine around their collective center of gravity. War Machine's grip on him loosened, and Tony took the opportunity to fling War Machine—with the unfortunate Rhodey inside, yelling all kinds of things on the HUD-to-HUD frequency—into the reflecting pool.

One of the gadgets he'd built into the Mark VI (despite being unconvinced he'd ever have a use for it) was a retractable spike.

"Sorry about this," he said to Rhodey as the War Machine suit hit the deck on its back. Tony aimed the spike directly at the base of the suit's neck.

Shling!

There. He started piping Jarvis's new software through the wiring in the spike and into the onboard network. War Machine went inert. Rhodey was talking—Tony could feel the vibrations through the spike—but no sound came through because the suit was down.

"Rebooting systems," Jarvis said smoothly.

About thirty seconds later, the War Machine suit came back online, system by system. Rhodey sat up, and Tony let him. They settled next to each other on the edge of the pool, enjoying a moment of peace and quiet. About a hundred cherry trees lined the edges of the pool and the paths that circled it and wound through the gardens. "Feeling better?" Tony asked after a bit.

"I'm so sorry," Rhodey said.

CHAPTER 16

With cherry blossoms drifting around them, Tony and Rhodey took a breather. But Tony knew he had to get moving. Natasha had told him Ivan was no longer at his workshop in the warehouse. Tony hoped S.H.I.E.L.D. was doing its job and would find Whiplash before he had to.

His thoughts were interrupted when the last remaining Army drone broke the peace and quiet he and Rhodey had been enjoying. It was slightly the worse for wear, with obvious repulsor burns and scoring on its armor, but it was moving on its own two feet to carry out its mission.

Tony opened the HUD-to-HUD with Rhodey. "Well," he said. "You ready to make it up to me?"

"I think we got this," Rhodey said. They stood facing the lone drone.

Then they heard a rumble, and blossoms began to shake loose from the trees. The rumble grew louder, its vibrations coming up through the soles of their boots. Sixteen more drones surrounded them. The Marines had arrived. So had the Navy. The reinforcements landed in a precise pattern, creating crossfire but keeping each other out of the planned field of fire.

The Army drone had come in first, and it took the initiative. With a ratcheting whine, a missile rack opened out of the drone's shoulders and snapped into position.

Tony didn't waste any time. He stepped up and reached out, tearing the rack from the drone's torso while it was still executing the firing routine. Before the drone could abort, Tony had turned around the launch tube. The missile fired, annihilating the robot's upper half and temporarily whiting out Tony's heads-up display.

He let the tube drop and said, "That's one."

❋◉☉

Pepper was crossing the Expo grounds, trying to find Agent Coulson. She had glimpsed him earlier and knew he and his S.H.I.E.L.D. agents were trying to help. She had seen the other drones take off in Tony's direction, and she wanted the agents to help *him*. She tried calling Tony again. He didn't answer. "Hi, this is Tony Stark, and you're Pepper Potts," said his voice mail. *Beeeeep.*

Pepper spotted Coulson ahead. She started to follow, putting her phone away; then she froze, still as a rabbit. With a flash of light and a crack that rang in her ears, Whiplash appeared in front of her.

Pepper looked past him, but Coulson had already gone into the milling crowds. Even if he'd heard Ivan, he was too far away to help. And this Ivan was different, not the invader from the Monaco racetrack. This Ivan was armored in a deranged parody of the Mark IV suit, gleaming like a gladiator, his hair loose and his face obscured behind a triangular mask. He loomed between her and safety.

"Congratulations on the new job," he said.

CHAPTER  17

Foom! One more Navy drone down. Rhodey was holding down one of the Marine drones as his weapons chewed through its armor.

"Ahoy, pal," Tony said, HUD to HUD. "I'm taking bets on whether we get this done before Ivan shows up to take advantage of us in our weakness."

"Well, now, that would be just like him to take advantage, wouldn't it?" Rhodey said.

They combined their fire on a Marine drone. Rhodey pinned it down and chewed it up with the big machine gun, and Tony finished it off. In the middle of this assault, Pepper called. Again.

Tony's lighthearted attitude evaporated the second he saw her face. She was mortally terrified. He could read her expression, even with the lousy resolution of the heads-up image. "Pepper?"

"Tony..." she said. And that's when the view shifted a bit, and he saw who else was there. He understood both her terror and why she had made the call.

"Where are you going?" Rhodey shouted, HUD to HUD, over the shriek of explosive projectiles from the diminishing number of drones. Tony counted two Marines and four Navy drones left. From seventeen to two, the odds had improved to six to one. Tony felt he had done his part.

"Keep them contained. Don't let them into the fairgrounds," Tony said, and thundered away.

❄◉☉

Fifteen seconds later, Tony landed in front of Whiplash and Pepper. The impact was hard enough to shake the ground and cause a momentary swirl of interference across his heads-up. Vanko held Pepper in one hand, lazily flicking a whip around her feet. She was clearly terrified, but Pepper Potts was also one tough customer. She stood straight.

Tony could see that Ivan had been busy. The villain had designed himself a new suit. He had graduated to armoring himself to protect his own limbs from his nasty whips. Of course, the whips were improved as well. They could be stored in spools that wrapped around the forearms. The whips deployed from slots at the insides of the wrists, and they could be controlled without the user holding them. It was as if the whips grew from Ivan, and he now used them not as tools but as extensions of his arms.

"Let her go before—" Tony started to say, and then stopped as Ivan released her. She scrambled away from him.

"Easy, wasn't it?" Ivan said. "You think I want her? No." *Snap!* went one of the whips. "I want only you."

"We still have a problem, then," Tony said.

Out came the full-length whips, crackling as they uncoiled and sparked to white-hot life, melting the asphalt on contact. When Vanko came at him with the whips, Tony grabbed hold of one and used it as a pivot to fling Ivan away, smashing him into a row of barriers. Vanko started to get up, and Tony covered the distance between them quickly.

The last time he had tangled with Ivan, Tony had been wearing the portable suit from the football, and Vanko had been using an experimental prototype of his whips and the armored frame that supported them. Now Tony was in the Mark VI, with a new RT and a new lease on life, and Vanko had taken a cue from Tony and armored up as well. Last time had been a dry run — this time was for real.

Ivan roared and went after Tony, who met him full on, exchanging punches for slashes of the whips. Tony found out quickly, though, that whatever Ivan was using this time around, it was a lot more powerful than the whips he'd had in Monaco.

"Pepper," he said, "get out of here!"

His train of thought was derailed as a whip cracked across the face shield of the Mark VI. His HUD flared and went dark. "Jarvis," Tony warned; as he spoke, the display went live again, and Ivan Vanko filled his field of vision.

"Divert to torso projector," Tony said. He felt the energy in the suit shift and then release in an enormous burst that blew Ivan through the nearest wall. In the brief lull that followed, Tony turned to Pepper. "I told you to get out of here, Pepper!" But she was frozen in place.

Ivan Vanko hit him in the small of the back and hammered him into the pavement hard enough to crack it. Tony spun, landing a solid elbow to the side of Vanko's head. Ivan flicked a whip that caught Tony's forearm, jerking it painfully backward. Tony rolled with the motion, scissoring Ivan's legs out from under him and stomping on the hand that held the whip. It uncoiled, and sparks shot from the forearm of Vanko's armor.

"Are we really doing this because of something

you think my dad did to your dad?" Tony asked. "And what was that thing, exactly? You think my dad stole the Arc Reactor idea, right? You've hurt innocent people. Is it their fault that your dad didn't get credit?" Tony shook his head. "It's nobody's fault but your own."

The next thing he knew, a whip snapped around his ankles. His feet were jerked out from under him. Whiplash landed on Tony's back and flicked a whip twice around Tony's neck. He caught the tip in one hand and closed his other around the base, where it came out of his wrist armor. Then Ivan hauled back with all his strength.

Tony could feel the heat from the whip through the armor around his neck. The HUD was flashing all kinds of red signals. The whips had damaged the suit's control systems. Tony couldn't get up. He couldn't really attack Ivan. And he couldn't hold the whip away from his neck forever.

There was one thing, however, that he could do. Letting go of the whip with one hand, he reached toward Pepper and triggered a hidden hatch in the gauntlet. It flicked open.

She was looking at him, horrified and paralyzed with fear. "Think fast," Tony said.

The Tech Ball shot out of the compartment behind the tiny forearm hatch. Instinctively, Pepper flung up her hand to catch it. In the milliseconds before it would have impacted the palm of her hand, the Tech-Ball adjusted the consistency of its material and changed shape, transforming from a metallic spheroid to a thin elastic hemisphere that closed around Pepper's hand and molded to its shape. Tony had been playing with the new invention and had created something more than just a fun toy.

A burst of repulsor energy exploded from the palm of Pepper's hand. The recoil knocked her back, and she stumbled and fell as the repulsor ray hit Ivan with a full-strength blast.

For a moment, nothing else changed. Vanko's arms still bulged with the strain of holding the whip around Tony's neck, and Tony's gauntleted fingers still sparked and smoked inside the tightening noose of the whip. Then, slowly, Vanko's arms relaxed. The whip loosened, and Tony jerked it away, letting it spit and crackle on the ground.

Tony stood, letting Ivan slump to the pavement. He flipped up the face shield of the Mark VI and winked at Pepper.

"Nice shot," he said.

"Thanks," Pepper said, gasping. Both of them stood there for a moment, recovering.

"How about we go home?" she asked.

He pulled off his helmet and smiled at her. "Sounds like a plan."